STILL WATER

CHRIS PRIESTLEY

Barrington Stoke

First published in 2018 in Great Britain by
Barrington Stoke Ltd
18 Walker Street, Edinburgh, EH3 7LP

www.barringtonstoke.co.uk

This edition first published 2019

Text & Illustrations © 2018 Chris Priestley

The moral right of Chris Priestley to be identified as the author
and illustrator of this work has been asserted in accordance with
the Copyright, Designs and Patents Act, 1988

A CIP catalogue record for this book is available
from the British Library upon request

ISBN: 978-1-911370-11-6

Printed and bound in Great Britain by
Clays Ltd, Elcograf S.p.A.

STILL WATER

Contents

Chapter 1

Leaving London

Rosie was finding it hard to listen to what her mother was saying. There was so much happening. There were too many thoughts in her head.

"But I don't want to go," Rosie said quietly as her mother hugged her.

"Now don't start all that again, Rosie," said her mother. "You have to go. It's all sorted.

Besides, what sort of a mother would I be if I didn't send you off to safety?"

"But—"

"You won't want to be here when the bombs start falling. You'll have wished you'd gone then, won't you?" her mother told her.

"But what about you?" Rosie said. "You hate loud noises more than me."

"I do," her mother agreed. "I do hate loud noises. I'm terrified at the thought of explosions, but we all have to be brave, don't we, and do what's best? We can't be selfish, can we? What would Dad say when he comes home? We all have to pull together till it's over. Now come on, give us a hug. You'll be back in no time."

Rosie stared at the label round her neck and her little suitcase and the box with the gas mask in, all done up with string as if it was a present. She hated the idea of leaving home, but her whole school was being evacuated to the countryside to protect them from the war that was about to come.

"Look – all your friends are there," said her mother. She pointed to the other children standing by the school gates.

But they weren't Rosie's friends. Not real friends. Rosie didn't mix that well at school. Just as her mum didn't mix that well with the other mothers. It didn't bother either of them that much. They liked their own company, that was all.

Rosie only really had one proper friend – Lucy Peters – and Lucy had already left London to go and stay with her aunt in Devon. But Rosie could see that her mother wanted to think everything was fine, so she said nothing. *Look after your mum for me*, her father had said as he left.

"Ready?" said a voice beside them. They both turned to see who it was and Rosie smiled when she saw it was Miss Baxter, her teacher.

"We're ready, aren't we, Rosie?" said her mother, and Rosie nodded.

Miss Baxter held out her hand and Rosie took it.

"Aren't the mothers going to the station?" said Rosie's mother, and her voice shook a little. Rosie hoped her mum wouldn't cry. She couldn't bear to see that.

"We thought it best if you said your goodbyes here at the school gate," Miss Baxter said. "Better for the children. Better for everyone."

Rosie could see her mother wasn't at all sure it was for the best. But she nodded, swallowed back a sob and gave Rosie one last hug.

"There's writing paper in your case," she said. "Don't you forget to write."

"I won't, Mum," said Rosie. "I promise," and she didn't cry until she got to the end of the street.

They walked all together to the station. It was a long way. They'd hardly been allowed to take anything, but Rosie's case already felt heavy and the stupid gas-mask box kept banging into her leg.

"Are you coming with us, miss?" one of the boys asked Miss Baxter, and Rosie was glad when the teacher answered that, yes, she was.

"Of course I'm coming too," Miss Baxter said. "Otherwise all the learning will leak out of your silly heads and you'll be like animals by the time you come back."

Rosie smiled. She liked Miss Baxter. At least there would be one friendly face.

People stared and pointed as Rosie and the others lined up on the platform to catch the train. There were children from other schools there too. Everyone was very excited about the train journey and even Rosie forgot some of her worries as they climbed the steps and edged into the packed carriages.

Rosie was lucky. She managed to squeeze through and get a seat next to the window. Lots of children had to stand in the corridor. The noise was deafening and a great cheer went up as the train pulled out of the station with a gasp of steam.

Rosie rested her head against the cold glass and tuned out the rest of the jabbering noise in the carriage. She watched the houses and offices and factories of London clatter by and give way to fields and rivers and open countryside. So many trees. She had never seen so many trees.

After what seemed an age, a lot of children were told they were to get off the train at the next station, but Miss Baxter came into Rosie's carriage to say that it wasn't their stop yet and she would tell them when it was.

As it turned out, they were the last to leave and the train was almost empty when Rosie finally stepped onto the platform along with the rest of the children from her school.

The teachers who had come with them made the children line up and then counted them to make sure they were all there, asking their names and checking them against a list they held in their hands.

There was a little group of women from the village on the platform to meet the children. They smiled at the teachers. But Rosie noticed they looked a little less sure of the children who had now come to live among them.

Then the teachers led the children away, out of the station and up a long road that led to the centre of the village, where there was a village green, a little stream, a cluster of houses, a shop, a pub and a gold cockerel weather vane shining at the top of the church tower. *It's like a picture from a children's story*, thought Rosie.

They were taken to the village hall, where they stood at one end and a group of women stood at the other end, whispering and pointing. In the middle of the hall, there was a desk with two women and a girl sitting at it.

"Shall we get started then?" said a woman who seemed to be in charge. "These youngsters have had a long day. Let's not keep them standing about."

Another woman stepped forward and, after looking from face to face, chose a girl to Rosie's left.

"Come with me," said the woman with a smile. "I won't bite."

"But I can't go without Frank!" the girl cried.

"Who's Frank?" asked the woman.

"He's my brother," said the girl. "I can't go without him. He's only little."

"Well ..." said the woman. She looked doubtful.

"Come on, Gwen," said the woman in charge. "You've got the room."

"All right," Gwen said. "We have to do our bit, don't we?"

"Indeed we do!" said the woman. "Now come on, everyone – let's speed this up a bit, shall we?"

After a moment or two the women moved forward and picked the child – or children –

they wanted to take home. But no one picked Rosie. She worried that no one was going to choose her, when a friendly looking woman tapped her on the arm. It was the woman who had been in charge. She was standing with the girl Rosie had seen earlier sitting at the desk.

"Here we are, my dear," she said. "Did you think we'd forgotten you? My name is Mrs Taylor."

"Hello. It's very kind of you to take me in," said Rosie, remembering the words her mother had told her to say.

Mrs Taylor stopped and smiled down at her.

"Well, you're very welcome, I'm sure," she said. "I'm sure your mother would do the same for my Mary if things were the other way round."

"Oh, she would," agreed Rosie. "My mum's very kind. Everyone says so."

"I'm sure she is, darling," said Mrs Taylor.

But Rosie noticed that a strange little look passed across Mary's face.

Chapter 2

Bitten

Mary held Rosie's hand all the way home and Rosie thought she must have been wrong about the funny look. The house where Mary and her mother lived looked like a fairy-tale cottage. It had fat chimneys and orange roof tiles, small windows and roses round the door.

Mary chatted away as she showed Rosie round the house and took her to meet the chickens and rabbits they kept in the back garden. Rosie loved the chickens – and the idea that they would lay eggs for her breakfast.

Mrs Taylor followed them about and told Mary to show this and that and explain such and such until Rosie was a little dizzy with the newness of it all.

Rosie even had her own room – a small but very cosy one at the back of the house. From the window, Rosie could see the garden and the woods beyond. It was a nice room with wallpaper patterned with hundreds of tiny flowers and a cast-iron bedstead with shiny brass bits here and there.

Rosie put her little case and gas-mask box on the bed and followed Mary back downstairs. Mrs Taylor put the radio on and said she had better get on with the cooking as it was getting late. Rosie watched Mrs Taylor walk away into the kitchen and suddenly felt very tired.

It was then that the look on Mary's face changed so much that Rosie asked her if she was all right. Mary leaned forward and said, in a low whispered voice, "I ... don't ... want ... you ... here!"

"What?" said Rosie.

"You heard me," said Mary. "We were fine on our own. Why should we have you living here?"

"Well ... I don't see what I can do about it," said Rosie.

To Rosie's amazement, Mary then raised her arm to her mouth and sank her teeth into the flesh. Then she stared back at Rosie and grinned. Rosie's heart skipped a beat.

With Rosie still watching, Mary stood up and kicked a chair over. Then she cried out – a sudden cry filled with pain. Tears sprang to her eyes and she moved back, away from Rosie as if Rosie was a monster. When Mrs Taylor walked in, Mary pointed at Rosie and screamed again.

"She bit me!" Mary howled.

"What?" Rosie said. "No I didn't."

Mrs Taylor was already looking at Mary's arm and gasped when she saw the teeth marks. She turned to Rosie with a frown.

"What on earth?" she said.

"She said I'd better do as she said or she'd bite me—" Mary sobbed.

"That ain't true!" Rosie shouted.

"And when I wouldn't say yes, she bit me!" Mary cried.

Mrs Taylor hugged her daughter and frowned at Rosie.

"I'm disgusted," she said. "I don't know how they behave in London, but round these parts we—"

"I didn't bloody do it!" Rosie yelled.

Mrs Taylor stared at her in shock.

"I think you'd better go to your room!" Mrs Taylor said.

Rosie opened her mouth to protest, but instead she stormed out of the door and up the stairs to her room. She threw herself on the bed, face down, and howled a scream of rage into the pillow.

*

Rosie lay there for a long time, curled around her case, and tried to remember every detail of her own home, remembering and remembering until it hurt too much.

Then there was a knock on the door and Mrs Taylor came in. She sat on the bed. Rosie didn't look round. Mrs Taylor put her hand on Rosie's arm and Rosie flinched.

"I had a long talk to Mary," Mrs Taylor said quietly. "I wanted you to be moved somewhere else. Because I can't have that sort of behaviour in my house. I thought you London children might be a bit rough round the edges, but that really is too much."

"But I didn't—"

"Never mind," said Mrs Taylor. "I don't want to hear about it. Mary says she forgives you and wants you to stay. So do I. I think all the business of being away from your mother has upset you. If you ever do anything like that again, I'll send you back no matter what Mary says, but I have a feeling you aren't really a bad girl. It's probably just the upset of leaving home and coming somewhere new and different. So why don't we try again?"

Rosie was so tired. This seemed the easiest way. To start again.

"Yes," said Rosie. "All right. Yes, please."

Mrs Taylor smiled.

"Good," she said. "That's all sorted then. I'll bring you up something to eat. It'll all seem better in the morning."

"I really didn't bite her you know," Rosie said.

"Now don't be silly, dear," Mrs Taylor said, turning back to Rosie as she opened the door. "She's hardly likely to bite herself, now, is she?"

*

Rosie felt a bit better after she had something to eat. She sat in her room and leafed through an old travel book she found on the bookshelves. It was full of pictures of faraway places and exotic people.

There were a number of little knocks on the door. Mary opened it and walked in. Rosie looked back at the book.

"You see," Mary said as she walked slowly over to the bed. "She believes me. She always believes me. So you'd better look out."

"Why not get me sent away?" Rosie said. "If you hate me so much."

"I was going to," Mary said. "Don't worry. But then I thought how much more fun it would be to have you here and know that all I have to do is yell and you'll get into trouble. You'll have to be careful."

"Maybe I'll just really bite you," Rosie said. "How about that? Maybe I don't want to live here."

"You wouldn't do that," Mary said with a sigh. "You're not the type."

With that, she turned and left the room.

Rosie was tempted to rush after Mary and bite her just to prove her wrong, but she knew in her heart that Mary was right after all. Rosie was just not that sort of girl.

Chapter 3

The Girl in the Water

The next morning, Rosie woke as the sunshine burst brightly through a gap in the curtains. For a moment or two, she forgot where she was and her heart raced in panic.

When she did remember, she didn't feel much better. She felt awkward and a little tense. She remembered Mary and the bite and the look on Mrs Taylor's face.

What time was it? She tried to work out how early it was by how hungry she felt, but she wasn't sure if the rumble in her stomach was hunger or worry.

Rosie got out of bed and wandered over to the window. She pulled one of the curtains aside and lifted the net curtain behind it. It was a clear, bright September day.

She could not remember ever seeing a morning so bright in London. The air here was so clear. She could see for miles, out across the meadow to the woods and the fields beyond.

There was a knock at her bedroom door and Mrs Taylor opened it a little. Her face was more friendly than Rosie might have hoped.

"Morning, dear," she said. "Would you like some breakfast?"

"Yes, please," said Rosie.

Rosie didn't know if she should get dressed or not, but decided that she should. When she went downstairs, she was glad of her decision because she found Mary was dressed and had already finished her breakfast.

"Here you are," said Mrs Taylor. "Sit yourself down and have a nice cup of tea."

Rosie sat down and Mrs Taylor put a boiled egg and some toast in front of her. Rosie thanked her, then picked up her spoon and tapped at the shell.

"So I hope you two have made up," said Mrs Taylor. "I'm having some of the Parish Council round and I don't want you two under my feet, so off out and play. And I don't want any more nonsense."

"No, Mrs Taylor," said Rosie.

"Of course not, Mum," said Mary. "Come on, Rosie. Let's go to the woods!"

Rosie knew she couldn't trust Mary. She had already seen how quickly she could switch moods. But off they went – for all the world like the best of friends. Rosie wondered if Mary had just been out of sorts because she didn't like having a stranger in her house. Perhaps she'd be different today. Perhaps she wasn't really bad at all.

But as soon as they were out of sight of the house, she changed back to bad Mary. She kept up a constant stream of spiteful remarks and threats until they came to a clearing in the woods where a big group of children were standing next to a den made out of fallen branches, with swings hanging from nearby trees.

Rosie recognised some of her classmates. A boy she sometimes sat next to waved at her and Rosie waved back. The village children looked like they had been waiting for Mary to arrive and a couple of them ran forward to greet her.

"What's her name?" one of them asked, and pointed to Rosie.

"Her name's Nosy," said Mary.

They laughed.

"Hello, Nosy!" said one of the village boys.

"Her name's Rosie," said the boy who had waved, but he spoke so softly that only Rosie herself could hear.

"Let's play soldiers!" said Mary, and there was a cheer.

At first they were going to play English and Germans but no one wanted to be Germans, so in the end they decided they would play Romans and Barbarians.

Mary and a village boy picked the sides and the London children were happy to go along with it – happy to play and forget about London. The village boy picked Rosie for his side but Mary shook her head and said, "Not her."

When all the children had been picked, Mary started to lay down the rules of the battle. Rosie stood there and stood there. How could they leave her out so completely? No one from her school said, "No – we can't play without Rosie." They just turned their backs on her and the two sides ran off in different directions into the woods. Rosie was left alone.

Rosie didn't want to walk straight back to the house. She didn't want to answer the questions she was sure Mrs Taylor would ask. Mrs Taylor did not want to hear the truth about her daughter and certainly did not want to hear it from Rosie.

Instead, Rosie made her way slowly to the centre of the village and watched the strangers go about their daily chores. It looked like a painting. How her mother would love it. She was always moaning about the noise and soot of London and dreaming of how they might one day move to the country. But Rosie missed the noise and the soot.

"Hello, dear," said a voice behind her, so suddenly it made her jump.

"Mrs Taylor," said Rosie. "I was just ... I was just ..."

Mrs Taylor smiled at her.

"You don't seem very sure what you're doing, now, do you?" she said.

Rosie smiled and shook her head.

"Where's Mary?" said Mrs Taylor, looking round. "I thought you'd be playing with the others. You haven't fallen out again, have you?"

"No ... no," said Rosie. "I just ... I wanted to be on my own for a bit."

Mrs Taylor sighed.

"Missing your mum, are you?" she said after a little while.

Rosie nodded. *I won't cry, I won't cry*, she thought to herself.

"Well, that's only natural," said Mrs Taylor. "I hope Mary would miss me if she was taken off somewhere. But it'd take your mind off it, wouldn't it?"

"What would take my mind off it, Mrs Taylor?" Rosie asked.

"Playing with the others."

"Oh – yes," said Rosie. "I suppose so."

The path went by an old mill pond. The mill looked as if it had been empty for years. There were big holes in the roof and a tree grew out of one of the walls.

As they approached the pond, Mrs Taylor took Rosie's hand in hers and walked on quickly. Rosie could feel the tension in Mrs Taylor's body and feel the grip on her hand tighten.

Rosie thought at first there was no one else around but as she turned to look at the mill pond, something broke through the surface and sent ripples across the dark water.

It was a girl. A girl about Rosie's age, with long black hair that swirled like oil around her face. Rosie stopped in her tracks and stared, but the girl shook her head and put a finger to her lips, and Rosie knew she meant that Rosie was not to tell.

"What?" said Mrs Taylor. "What are you looking at?"

Rosie looked back at the pond and there was no sign of the girl, not even a ripple to show she'd ever been there.

"Nothing," said Rosie. "I thought I saw a ... fish."

"A fish?" said Mrs Taylor. "You have to have good eyesight to see a fish from up here."

She chuckled and they walked on, with Rosie secretly wondering who that mysterious girl might be. *Maybe she will be my friend*, thought Rosie.

Chapter 4

The Witches' Pond

Rosie was still thinking about the girl in the pond when Mary came home and they all had lunch together.

"I hope you're helping Rosie to make friends," said Mrs Taylor.

"Oh, she is," said Rosie, before Mary could say anything.

Mary smiled. Rosie didn't.

"Well, I'm pleased to hear it," said Mrs Taylor as she busied herself round the kitchen.

"It's still so warm," said Rosie.

Mary rolled her eyes.

"It's going to get even warmer, they say," said Mrs Taylor. "Too hot for me, I must admit."

"Me and my mum go swimming when it's hot," said Rosie. "In the London Fields Lido. They've closed it down now on account of the war that's coming."

"The war will be over before you know it," said Mrs Taylor kindly. "It'll be open again just like before, I'm sure."

Rosie nodded. Mrs Taylor was probably right. They would open it again after the war.

If it wasn't bombed. *But it will never be the same*, thought Rosie. Nothing would. She was suddenly sure of that.

"Cheer up, dear," said Mrs Taylor, seeing Rosie's face. "Things are never as bad as you think."

Mary smiled again. Her special cruel smile she never let her mother see.

"Would it be all right if I went for a swim here?" Rosie asked. "In that mill pond we saw? I've brought my costume. We could all go."

Mrs Taylor stopped and stared at her.

"The Witches' Pond?" she said.

"Is that what it's called?" said Rosie. "The Witches' Pond? That's a funny name."

"Funny name?" said Mrs Taylor, still staring at her.

"No one ever swims there," said Mary.

Rosie was about to tell Mary about the girl she'd seen, when she remembered how the girl had silently begged her not to tell.

"Why?" Rosie asked.

"Because ..." began Mrs Taylor. "Because it's ... well ... it's got a bad history."

"What kind of bad history?" Rosie asked.

"Oh my, but you ask a lot of questions. Has anyone ever told you that?" Mrs Taylor said.

Rosie thought that this would be the end of the conversation, but Mrs Taylor sighed and went on.

"Well, they call it the Witches' Pond on account of how they once ducked seven witches there on a single day."

"Ducked?" asked Rosie.

"It was a test," Mrs Taylor said. "A cruel test for witches. Back in olden times. They tied you up and tossed you in the water. If you floated, then you were a witch and they hanged you. If you sank, well, then you were innocent. Five of them drowned. The two that were said to have floated were hanged."

Rosie shuddered as she pictured the scene. Mrs Taylor shook her head and sighed again. "What would your mother say if she heard me filling your head with such terrible things?"

"My mum says grown-ups should always try to be honest with children," Rosie told her.

"Does she now?" said Mrs Taylor with a little frown.

"And is that why no one swims there?" Rosie said. "Because of the witches that drowned there all those years ago. But what if—"

"No," said Mrs Taylor, her voice a little more strained than before. "Not just that. It's worse than that, though that would be bad enough, I'm sure. No – a girl was drowned there. When I was only a girl myself. She was told not to swim there – we all were – and she drowned. No one has swum there since."

"Really? But how did she—"

"I think we've talked about this enough now," said Mrs Taylor, raising her voice. "You'll be having nightmares."

Rosie frowned at the idea that she would be so scared, but let it pass.

"So there we are," said Mrs Taylor, more gently now and forcing a smile. "You mustn't go swimming there. We wouldn't want anything to happen to you here in the countryside now, would we? You've come to get away from danger, haven't you?"

Rosie smiled and nodded. But all the same, she still wanted to swim. The girl in the mill pond hadn't looked like she was in any kind of danger. It all sounded like what her mother would have called a "load of old nonsense".

Chapter 5

At the Pond

After lunch, Rosie was once again sent to play with Mary by Mrs Taylor. Rosie could hardly complain, as she had told her that everything was just fine. The afternoon was pretty much the same as the morning.

Rosie was surprised at how much effort Mary put into ignoring her. She could see that Mary spent almost all of her time thinking about it. Rosie saw her take quick sideways looks just to check that Rosie was still being shunned.

In a strange way, it made Rosie feel a little better. The fact that Mary was making such a big show of ignoring Rosie just made Mary look silly and small.

But even so, it was no fun being kept on the outside of everything, and no fun at all to have Mary tell lies about her. Rosie saw her show the bite mark to the other children and then point over to Rosie.

At first she felt like she ought to stay and tough it out – to show she wasn't beaten – but in the end it just became too boring and she wandered off. She noticed the crooked smile on Mary's face as she left.

Rosie thought of her mother and her house and her street. Tears stung her eyes but she was determined not to cry. She sniffed and blinked and walked on, her chin thrust out.

Then, as Rosie came out of the wood, she saw the same girl swimming in the centre of the mill pond. She waved at Rosie again and Rosie waved back.

"Come in," said the girl. "It's a bit cold at first but you get used to it."

Rosie shook her head.

"I'm not allowed," she said. "It's dangerous."

The girl laughed.

"Dangerous?" she said. "Does it look dangerous?"

"Well ..." said Rosie. "But Mrs Taylor says—"

"Oh, you don't want to listen to her," said the girl.

"You know Mrs Taylor?" asked Rosie.

The girl nodded.

"Do you live near here?" said Rosie.

The girl's smile vanished. Even in the shadow of the trees, her eyes shone and sparkled as if they were lit from inside. Rosie felt a little dizzy looking at them.

"Why are you on your own?" asked the girl. "Don't you have any friends?"

"They won't let me play," said Rosie. "The other children. They ignore me."

"Don't let them make you unhappy, Rosie," she said.

"How do you know my name?" asked Rosie.

"I know what it's like," said the girl, ignoring Rosie's question. "I'm lonely too."

"Really?" said Rosie. "Don't you have any friends either?"

"I used to have one really special friend," said the girl. "But then ..."

The girl didn't finish her sentence and looked down sadly at her own reflection in the rippling water.

"I miss her," said the girl quietly.

"Did she move away?" asked Rosie.

But the girl didn't reply. Rosie stood there for a while, not knowing what to say.

"I'm sorry," she said at last, but the girl didn't even look up. Rosie couldn't see her face now, she was so bent over. She could only see the top of her head and the thin pale parting in her black hair which spread out around her on the surface of the dark grey water.

When the girl finally did look up again, she had a smile on her face.

"Bring Mary next time," she said.

"Mary?" said Rosie. "Mary Taylor?"

The girl nodded.

"She doesn't like me," said Rosie. "She wouldn't do anything I asked."

"Try," said the girl.

Rosie was hurt that this girl wanted Mary. How could Rosie be friends with anyone who liked Mary?

"Try," repeated the girl.

"I'd better go," said Rosie. "I'll ask her, but she won't listen to me."

The girl nodded and Rosie began to walk away.

"Wait," said Rosie. "I don't even know your name."

But when Rosie turned back, the girl was gone. The Witches' Pond was flat and black once more, with not so much as a ripple on its surface.

Chapter 6

Not You

Rosie walked back to the children. She had nowhere else to go. When she got there, they had broken up into groups. She hung around on the edge of things again. No one even seemed to notice she was there at first.

Then the boy from her school in London who had waved at her came over.

"I'm Paul," he said.

She nodded.

"Where have you been?" he asked.

"Nowhere really," said Rosie. "Just to the pond on the other side of the trees. There was a girl swimming there. We got talking."

"A girl?" said one of the village boys, overhearing them. "But all the girls in the village are here. Everyone's here."

Rosie blushed a little.

"Well, there was," she insisted. "I talked to her."

The other children began to gather around.

"What are you talking about?" asked Mary, walking forward.

"She says she saw a girl in the Witches' Pond," said the village boy.

"Liar," said Mary. "No one swims there."

"Why would I lie?" said Rosie.

"Habit, I expect," said Mary, and some of the children laughed.

"Maybe it was one of the evacuees," said one of the boys.

"They're all here as well," said Mary. "Don't take any notice of her."

"I don't care," said Rosie. "I know what I saw."

"How could you have seen anyone?" said Mary. "There was no one to see."

"Maybe it was a ghost?" joked a girl with a mass of freckles all over her face and arms.

"A ghost?" said Rosie. "No, I—"

"My mum says she saw a ghost once," said another of the boys.

He did an impression of a floating ghost, eyes wide and arms outstretched. One of the girls squealed and they all laughed.

"She's just making it up," said Mary. "My mum told her about the girl who drowned."

"I'm not making it up," said Rosie. "I never said she was a ghost. She was just a girl."

But even as Rosie said it, she remembered the shining eyes. She felt a little dizzy all of a sudden.

"Look at her," said Mary. "You can see she's lying."

"It's true!" said Rosie. "She even asked me to …"

Rosie opened her mouth to carry on but nothing came out. Why should she pass on the message to Mary? If the girl wanted Mary to come there so much, she could ask Mary herself. Rosie just shook her head and turned away.

After a moment, all the children got back to what they were doing before. It was like a wall went up between them and Rosie, and she felt like she could have shouted and shouted and no one would hear her.

Rosie walked off towards the woods, hoping that none of them had seen the tears that were already running down her face, and when she felt she was far enough away she stood behind a tree and folded her arms across her face so that no one would hear her sobs. When she had finished, she kicked and kicked and kicked out at a tree in anger, wishing it was Mary.

Why did she care so much what Mary or any of them thought? She had never really been bothered at school. She was just happy sitting on her own. She realised that although she hadn't cared if she played with the other children, she liked having them there. Now Mary seemed to have infected the others with her nastiness. Or maybe they had always been like that and she had never noticed.

Rosie thought of the girl at the pond. Could she really be a ghost? But ghosts were from the past and the girl knew Mary and Mrs Taylor. Rosie closed her eyes and tried to remember her face, but it was like trying to remember a dream.

*

Rosie was pulled back towards the pond. She felt her heart racing as she walked. A breeze played among the branches, and the trunks of the smaller trees swayed and creaked. She wanted to run back to the others, but it felt as if she had no choice but to carry on, even though she didn't know what she might find. But there was no sign of the girl at the pond.

Rosie looked back towards the woods and the other children, then at the still waters of the pond, then back to the woods. She had thought she might feel relief when she found the pond empty, but instead she felt disappointed and sad.

The girl was the only person in this whole place who had spoken to her with any kindness. There was something sad about her and Rosie wanted to know why. She had to know why. Her fear was flowing away. She just wanted to see the girl again.

*

Rosie went back to the house. There was no one in, but the back door was open. She went upstairs and put her swimming costume on under her clothes, found a towel and went back to the pond.

Rosie felt sure that this girl needed a friend as much as Rosie did, and Rosie would prove to her that she would make a better one than Mary. She took her clothes off behind a tree and then edged towards the water. Then she sat on the bank and let her feet slip under the surface. She gasped a little at the cold and decided to slide in before she changed her mind.

The girl was right, the pond seemed freezing at first, but when Rosie finally summoned up courage to put her whole body under the water, it felt wonderful to gaze up at the pale blue of the sky. She floated off on her back, the water twinkling around her.

She closed her eyes and imagined she was in the London Fields Lido, but it would never have been so quiet. It was always packed and noisy, and people would have been splashing and shouting and bumping into her.

She tried to imagine it closed and locked up. What a sad thing it must be. And while she was thinking this, the girl – the mystery girl from the pond – came into her thoughts again. The sense of unease came back too, and she stopped swimming and began to tread water in the centre of the pool.

Who was she? If all the village girls had been in the woods, who could the girl in the pond be? Maybe it was all a trick. Maybe Mary had put someone up to it – to pretend to be the ghost – just so Rosie would come and tell them. Then everyone could have a good laugh.

But Rosie knew in her heart that Mary really had been surprised when Rosie told them about the girl in the pond. So had the other children. This was no trick.

Then Rosie became aware that the birds were no longer singing. There was no sound at all. She looked up at the trees. They were still now. It was like being in a photograph. It was so quiet, she shook her head, thinking that she must have got water in her ears, but she realised that she could hear her own movements in the water well enough. It was everywhere else that was silent.

A cloud passed over the sun, and the mill pond went suddenly dark. A chill breeze skimmed the surface of the water and scattered goose bumps across Rosie's pale skin.

She shivered. And not just with the cold. She no longer felt safe. Perhaps everyone was right. Perhaps it was dangerous to swim here. She could feel the fear rising up in her, taking control of every part of her. She struggled to stay calm and swim for the bank. She climbed out and sat panting on the damp grass. Then she heard a voice.

"Not you."

The voice was whispered and loud at the same time. Rosie turned round, but there was no one there.

"Not you," said the voice again.

Rosie swallowed hard and held back tears as she quickly dried and dressed herself. Then she stood looking back at the mill pond, peaceful and lovely once more, the sun shining again. As she dried her hair with the towel, she saw a woman standing on the other side of the pond. When she noticed Rosie looking at her, she walked on.

Rosie had a pretty good idea where the woman was heading.

Chapter 7

Bad Dreams

Rosie had waited in the September sunshine, trying to dry her hair completely before walking into the house, but she could tell straight away that Mrs Taylor knew where she had been.

For a while, she said nothing, but when Rosie said she was going to her room to read, Mrs Taylor slapped her hand down on the table and made Rosie jump.

"You promised me you would not swim in that pond!" shouted Mrs Taylor. "Then I have Mrs Fellowes telling me she saw you!"

Rosie could have pointed out that actually she had made no such promise, but she could see by the way Mrs Taylor was looking at her that it would not be a good idea. She had found with her own mother that the best thing to do was just let her say her piece. It would all be over quicker.

But it soon became clear that Mrs Taylor was not like Rosie's mother, who would have one angry outburst and then just get over it. No – Mrs Taylor was not going to let this pass quite so easily.

"Go to your room!" she said. "Go on. Out of my sight!"

Rosie stood for a second or two, trying to think of what to say. Then she turned and ran up the stairs as if she was fleeing from a

chasing dog. She fumbled at the door handle
and then rushed into her room and slammed
the door behind her.

Rosie didn't cry. She thought she would
but she didn't. She just ached – ached with an
urge to be away from here and back with her
mother. She was angry with everything that
stopped her – Mary, Mrs Taylor, Miss Baxter –
the war, even. The war most of all.

But the thing that fixed itself most firmly
in her mind was that whispered "Not you."
It seemed to sum up her whole life at that
moment.

*

Rosie lay on the bed and flicked through books
without really taking in any of the words. And
then it began to get dark. Instead of putting

the light on, she simply lay back and closed her eyes.

Mrs Taylor came up with some food. She said very little to Rosie. Rosie thought she might tell her off again but she didn't. Somehow this was worse. It felt like Mrs Taylor was disappointed with her, but what right had she to be disappointed? What right had she to be anything? She wasn't Rosie's mother.

By the time Mary knocked on the door, Rosie was calm. She knew it was Mary. She did not respond, but Mary came in anyway and shut the door softly behind her.

"We told you not to go swimming in the Witches' Pond," Mary said.

"Leave me alone," said Rosie.

Mary chuckled. "I have been leaving you alone, silly," she said. "You're not very popular, are you? Maybe it's all the lying you do.

Saying you saw a ghost. You must think we're stupid."

"I didn't say I'd seen a ghost," said Rosie.

"Liar," said Mary.

"I hate you," said Rosie quietly.

"I know," said Mary. "I don't care. It's not my fault you've come here. You could have stayed in London and got bombed for all I care. I hope your mother—"

"Everything all right?" said Mrs Taylor, suddenly appearing in the doorway.

Mary changed immediately and smiled back at her mother.

"Yes, Mum," she said. "Just talking about what we'll do tomorrow."

Rosie saw that Mrs Taylor was giving Mary a strange look. How much had she heard before she spoke? Mary seemed to be thinking the same thing and her smile faded a little.

"Off to bed, Mary," said her mother.

Mary left the room without looking back.

"You too, Rosie. Off to sleep."

"Yes, Mrs Taylor," said Rosie.

But Rosie's sleep was full of dreams of the dark water of the Witches' Pond and a mysterious shape moving silently below the surface.

Chapter 8

Sunday

Early next morning, Mrs Taylor announced they were all off to church. Rosie and her mother didn't really go to church, but she did not feel it was the time to say. Mary was very quiet and wouldn't look at her.

They stopped off on the way to pick up Mrs Taylor's mother. She was very frail and seemed a little confused about who Rosie was, even though Mrs Taylor tried to explain. Rosie smiled at her, but the old lady frowned back and wouldn't talk to her.

Rosie looked around the church when they arrived. It seemed as if all the children were there, evacuees and villagers. Not Miss Baxter though.

The vicar seemed a kind man. He smiled a lot and told everyone they should welcome the "strangers in their midst" and make sure that they kept them safe for their parents back in London.

Afterwards, they took Mrs Taylor's mother back to her house, and when they got home Mrs Taylor nodded at Rosie to go upstairs. Rosie didn't mind. She felt less lonely on her own. She closed her bedroom door. She heard Mary and Mrs Taylor's voices in the hall, and then it went quiet as the door to the sitting room was closed.

It was so still. London was never still – not even on the rainiest Sunday. Rosie could just hear the voices of the Taylor family seeping up through the floor and she was amazed to hear the ticking of the clock in the hall downstairs. There was a bird twittering outside in the garden.

She felt a sudden urge to cry but swallowed it with a sigh. Instead, she pulled her suitcase from under her bed and found the pack of writing paper and a pencil her mother had given her. She began to write a letter:

Dear Mum

I hate it here!! I'm sad all the time. Please, please, PLEASE bring me home. Everyone is horrible. The girl here is mean to me and then blames me when her mum comes. She bit herself and blamed me. She is a liar and I hate her. There is nothing to do and

But she did not continue. How could she send a letter like that to her mother? It would only upset her, and she was probably already sad without Rosie there. It wasn't like her mum was having a good time either, and her father would be really angry if he saw it. No – if her mother could cope with the bombs and being on her own, then Rosie could cope with this.

She screwed up the paper and tossed it into the waste-paper bin, then got up and wandered over to the window and looked out into the garden. There was someone standing at the back gate. It was the girl from the Witches' Pond.

The girl stared up at Rosie with her shining eyes, and Rosie realised with a shudder that the girl was dripping wet, as though she had just stepped out of the pond, and was still wearing her swimming costume. Water dripped down the wooden gate and trickled down the path towards the house.

"Rosie!" came Mrs Taylor's voice from downstairs.

Rosie jumped and then went to her bedroom door and pulled it open. Mrs Taylor was in the hall shouting, "Come down – quick!"

"Coming," called Rosie.

When she looked back to the garden, the girl was gone. Rosie hurried down the stairs, and Mrs Taylor ushered her into the sitting room.

"Turn it up, Mary," Mrs Taylor said, and Mary reached over to the radio. The radio crackled and hissed, getting louder and louder.

It was the Prime Minister, Mr Chamberlain.

"I am speaking to you from the Cabinet Room of 10 Downing Street," he said. "This morning the British Ambassador in Berlin handed the German government a final note, stating that unless we heard from them by eleven o'clock that they were prepared at once to withdraw their troops from Poland, a state of war would exist between us. I have to tell you now that no such undertaking has been received and that, consequently, this country is at war with Germany."

Mrs Taylor put her arms round both girls.

"Well, then," she said. "I suppose we knew it would happen, and now it has. Now it has ..."

After a moment, she added, "Everything will be all right, girls. You'll see."

Here, maybe, thought Rosie. *But what about London? What about my mum? What about my dad?*

Chapter 9

A Walk Round the Village

Rosie went back to her room. After the radio announcement, Mrs Taylor seemed to have forgotten that Rosie was supposed to be shut away there in disgrace, but Rosie wanted to be on her own anyway. Her head was spinning. What was going to happen now?

Then Rosie remembered the girl from the pond, standing by the gate. She looked out of the window but there was no sign of her –

not even of the pool of water she had been standing in. The thought of the girl made Rosie feel dizzy, and deep down she knew that was because there was something not right about her. But how could she tell herself she had seen – spoken to – a ghost? It was too hard to believe.

The memory of the girl standing there, dripping wet, hair coiling round her shoulders like eels, was so strange that Rosie had already begun to believe she had imagined it. Once again, it seemed to fade like a dream as she walked back to sit on the bed. Maybe the girl wasn't a ghost. Maybe she was something in Rosie's head. Maybe she was imagining her. That seemed scarier somehow.

Rosie lay down and closed her eyes, thinking of her mum and dad and trying to imagine what they were doing right at that moment. She held them in her mind for as long as she could, and when they started to fade she followed them into the fog of sleep.

"Rosie?" said a faint voice.

"Mum?" murmured Rosie.

"Rosie?" came the voice again.

But it wasn't her mum. Rosie opened her eyes and saw that it was Mrs Taylor standing over her.

"Oh," said Rosie, sitting up. "Sorry ... I must have dozed off ... I ..."

Rosie was still half-asleep, so it took her a little while to notice that Mrs Taylor was holding a piece of paper – a crumpled piece of paper. It was Rosie's letter – the one she had thrown away.

"I was emptying your bin and this fell out ..." said Mrs Taylor.

"That was private," said Rosie, blushing a little.

"I know," said Mrs Taylor. "I'm sorry – I shouldn't have looked. But I'm glad I did."

Rosie peered at her.

"Glad?" she said. "Why?"

"Not glad exactly," said Mrs Taylor, coming over and sitting on the bed. "I just … Well, I'm sorry you feel so sad and very sorry you came close to telling your poor mother what a terrible time you're having here."

"I couldn't tell her," said Rosie. "That's why I threw it away."

"You're a good girl, Rosie," said Mrs Taylor.

"Not really," said Rosie. "Not especially. But I'm not a liar."

Mrs Taylor nodded.

"Mary's gone out to play, but I'll be having a word with her when she gets back."

"Please don't," said Rosie. "It'll make things worse. She'll just hate me all the more."

"I'm sure she doesn't hate you, dear," said Mrs Taylor.

Rosie was sure she did but bit her lip.

"I only wish the other children didn't just do whatever she does," said Rosie. "They could make their own minds up, couldn't they?"

"Well, that might just change," said Mrs Taylor. "Mrs Armstrong tells me you're a bit of a celebrity."

"Me?" said Rosie. "Why?"

"Oh – they've all heard how you went swimming in the Witches' Pond. They might not think you're so boring now."

Rosie had not said "boring". Was that how Mrs Taylor saw her? Did Rosie seem boring? Mrs Taylor seemed to sense her mistake.

"I was a bit like you when I was a girl," Mrs Taylor said.

Rosie didn't think that could have been true but thought it best to just listen.

"I was quiet," continued Mrs Taylor. "I found it hard to make friends ..."

Rosie blushed again. She did not like being talked about like this.

"It was a terrible thing," said Mrs Taylor, "when that girl drowned in the Witches' Pond. It was a really terrible thing. We all knew her of course. It's a small place. It's a shocking thing to happen when you're young. I still think about it now.

"I didn't want to frighten you. Or at least not just for the sake of it. I just wanted you to see why it's so important that you don't swim there."

Rosie nodded.

"I'm sorry," said Rosie. "I didn't mean anything by it. I didn't want to upset you or make you remember. I feel really bad about it now."

"I know," said Mrs Taylor. "We don't have to talk about it any more. I just need to hear a promise from you that you won't go swimming in the Witches' Pond again."

Rosie nodded.

"I promise," she said.

Mrs Taylor smiled and got to her feet.

"Well, then," she said. "How about we go for a walk? I expect you'd like a bit of fresh air after being cooped up in here?"

Rosie smiled.

"Yes. I'd like that."

So Mrs Taylor and Rosie went for a walk through the village, and on the way they met Rosie's teacher, Miss Baxter, looking very pale and hunched over.

"Hello, Rosie," she said, her voice thin and husky. Then she turned to Mrs Taylor and said, "Sorry, we haven't been introduced ..."

"Mrs Taylor."

"How do you do?" wheezed Miss Baxter.

"You don't sound at all well," said Mrs Taylor.

"Oh, I'll be fine," said Miss Baxter. "It's just a—" But she didn't finish her sentence because she broke out into a hacking cough.

"Perhaps you ought to be inside, my dear," said Mrs Taylor.

"I think you may be right," said Miss Baxter, looking worse than ever. "I had planned to take the children to the ruins of the old castle and—"

Miss Baxter collapsed into coughing again.

"Oh dear," she said when the coughing stopped. "I've been sent with the children to look after them."

"But school doesn't start for a while yet, does it?" said Mrs Taylor.

"That's right," said Miss Baxter. "Late on account of the war. But we can't have them running wild. They're good children, but they will get into mischief if they have nothing to do."

Even Rosie had to admit this was true.

"Well, I think we may be able to help there," said Mrs Taylor. "The children from the village help with the harvest. Would your London children like to do the same?"

"Oh, I'm sure they'd love to, wouldn't you, Rosie?" Miss Baxter said.

Rosie nodded – although she had no real idea of what that meant.

"It's hard work, mind you," said Mrs Taylor. "They'll sleep well."

Miss Baxter started coughing again.

"Now you really must get off to bed," Mrs Taylor said. "Have Mrs Peters make you some of her nice broth. It works like magic."

"Thank you," said Miss Baxter. "I will. How are you, Rosie? Have you settled in all right?"

Rosie looked quickly at Mrs Taylor.

"Yes," she said. "I've settled in really well, thanks, miss."

"Good," said Miss Baxter, coughing again. "Bye then."

Rosie and Mrs Taylor walked on, and just as they were close to the house again, Mrs Taylor put her arm on Rosie's arm.

"You don't have to stay in your room any more. You go and play with Mary and the others."

"I don't think they like me," said Rosie.

"Well then, they just haven't got to know you properly," said Mrs Taylor.

Rosie smiled weakly and followed Mrs Taylor into the house.

"I'm sorry I swam in the pond," said Rosie as they took their shoes off. "But there was a girl there you see and—"

"A girl?" said Mrs Taylor.

Her face had turned white and she took a step back to steady herself, reaching out to rest against the wall.

"Yes," said Rosie. "She was swimming. She asked me not to tell. No one knows who she is, but she knew who you were. And she knew who Mary was. They say she's a ghost. Do you believe in ghosts, Mrs Taylor?"

Mrs Taylor stared at her.

"She ... she knew Mary?" said Mrs Taylor.

"Yes," said Rosie. "She wanted me to bring her to the pond."

Mrs Taylor looked pale, and Rosie could see her hand trembling.

"Are you all right?" said Rosie.

"Yes ... Yes ... Of course," she said. "Just a little tired I think. I might be coming down with what your teacher's got."

But Rosie noted that Mrs Taylor had not answered her question about believing in ghosts.

Chapter 10

Talk of Ghosts

Rosie could sense a change in Mary the next day. Maybe Mrs Taylor had spoken to her after all. Or perhaps Mary could see that her mother knew about some of the mean things she'd done to Rosie. When Mrs Taylor told the girls to go out to play, Mary was only too happy to agree.

Mary did not even say anything as they walked together through the woods. She was clearly thinking about how to handle this new situation. Rosie had been sure that Mary would be mean to her again as soon as they were far away from the house. Somehow it was worse when they kept on walking in silence.

The other children greeted Rosie like a prisoner they were really happy to see free again. The children from her school were particularly keen to be seen to be on good terms with the girl who had swum in the Witches' Pond – now that they had all been told what a big thing it was. All their previous nastiness was forgotten and Rosie was happy to start again as if nothing had happened.

Rosie was amazed to see that Mary joined in with everyone else. Mary saw how everything was different now and knew she had to keep in with the others. Rosie was popular and Mary had to pretend to be happy to stand beside her "friend".

"Mary says a friend of her mother's drowned there when she was a girl," said one of Rosie's classmates.

Rosie smiled. Mary had been quick to make sure everyone was aware she knew all about the Witches' Pond. She wanted to be at the centre of everything.

"That's right," said Rosie.

"Were you frightened?" said another. "When you swam? Was it scary?"

"Why would I be frightened?" said Rosie as boldly as she could. "It's just an old pond."

"But weren't you scared of seeing the ghost again?" said one of the village girls.

"I don't know," said Rosie, shivering a little at the sudden memory of how cold the water was. "I don't think so."

"Because it wasn't a ghost," said Mary. "That's why. Anyway – all that's nonsense and you know it."

"Well ..." began one of the boys.

"Have you seen it?" said Mary, now ignoring Rosie and talking to the boy who had just spoken. "Have you seen the ghost?"

The boy shook his head and had to admit he hadn't.

"Anyone?" said Mary.

No one had.

"Well, who was it then?" said one of the boys.

"How would I know," she said. "It wasn't me that saw her."

"For all your talk, I don't see you swimming in the pond, Mary Taylor," said one of the village girls.

This was greeted with a murmur that rippled through the crowd of children.

"So?" said Mary.

"So if there's no ghost and you're not scared, why have you never been in?" one of the boys asked.

"Why would I want to go swimming in that smelly old pond?" said Mary. "Besides, we're not allowed."

"That's never stopped you before," said the girl to more murmuring.

The children were not impressed by this argument and Mary could tell. So could Rosie, and she smiled to see Mary feeling uncomfortable. Mary's face reddened with anger.

"All right. Let's all go for a swim in the stupid Witches' Pond!" she said. "Rosie can lead the way."

"No," said Rosie. "I promised your mother I wouldn't."

This was greeted with mutters and frowns by all apart from Mary.

"What?" said Mary. "You're not afraid of my mum, are you?"

"It's not that I'm scared of her," said Rosie. "I just promised, that's all."

Rosie could tell that this was not what they had expected her to say. This new promise-keeping Rosie was not much better than the old lying Rosie they had shunned.

"So?" said Mary.

Rosie shrugged.

"No," she said. "I'm not going to do it."

"All right," said Mary. "Let's go. If Rosie is too scared, she can stay here. Who cares anyway?"

"I'm not scared," said Rosie. "How can I be scared? I went on my own, remember?"

But no one really cared what Rosie was saying any more. Everything was back to how it had been before. Mary was back in charge and they all knew it.

"Everyone go home for your swimming stuff and we'll meet at the pond in twenty minutes," Mary said.

But Rosie could see that it had cost Mary a lot to regain her power. Mary could not hide

how she was feeling inside. She really was
scared of going against her mother – but more
than that, Rosie felt sure she was scared of
going to the Witches' Pond.

Chapter 11

Mrs Taylor Confesses

Rosie walked back towards the village. She was not as upset as she had been before when she was left out. This time she felt bad – guilty even.

She felt it was her fault for having put the whole idea of the Witches' Pond into everyone's head. Now Mary was going to get in trouble, and Rosie was to blame.

Rosie didn't really care about Mary. But she did care about Mrs Taylor, and she wondered what her own mother would think of her behaviour and felt a little ashamed. But what could she do about it now?

By now Rosie was standing outside the back door of the Taylors' house. She stared at the door handle for a long time before she grabbed hold of it and let herself in.

Straight away, she heard a strange sound. It was coming from Mrs Taylor, who was standing at the kitchen sink, hunched over, sobbing great heaving sobs that sent tremors all through her body.

Rosie was shocked and began to edge her way out of the kitchen. She hoped Mrs Taylor hadn't seen her.

"Don't," said Mrs Taylor. "Don't go."

Rosie stopped. Mrs Taylor turned, red-eyed.

"I've not been honest with you," said Mrs Taylor. "I've not been honest with anyone for a long time."

"About what?" said Rosie.

"About me and Vera."

"Who's Vera?" asked Rosie.

"The girl that drowned," said Mrs Taylor. "Her name was Vera. I didn't just know her. We were best friends."

Rosie stared at her.

"I don't know why I'm telling you this," said Mrs Taylor. "You, a little girl I hardly know. But there's something about you. I can't say what it is. And I will tell those that need to know, but I need to tell you first. Can I do that?"

Rosie nodded, but she felt frightened. She was suddenly scared of this woman and wanted more than ever to be home with those she knew and loved. Mrs Taylor dried her eyes and sat down at the kitchen table. Rosie sat down too.

"Oh, we were such close friends, Vera and me. Everyone said so. Then one day Vera just decided she wasn't my friend any more. We went from being the closest of close to never speaking a word to each other. Overnight. Can you imagine what that was like?"

Rosie tried to imagine, but she couldn't. She had never had a close friend like that.

"It was terrible," Mrs Taylor went on. "I cried and cried. We always said we'd be friends for ever. For ever. My mother fetched the doctor it was so bad. I couldn't sleep. I wouldn't eat. I'd begged her, you see, and she just laughed at me. Laughed! It was like she hated me all of a sudden. Then seeing Mary behaving like that towards you ... it was just like Vera all over again. I suppose it brought it all back. That and your asking about the Witches' Pond."

Mrs Taylor said nothing for a little while.

"When Vera stopped being my friend, she would cross the road to avoid me. You can see what a small place this is. Every day – more than once – I would have this reminder of how she was treating me and how different everything was now.

"For a long time, I was just upset. I would cry, and Vera seemed to enjoy it when I did, which made me cry all the more, of course. After a while, I stopped crying and began to hate her."

Mrs Taylor stared off into the distance for a while.

"It must have still been very sad when she died," said Rosie.

Mrs Taylor looked at her. It was a strange look.

"There were always stories about the Witches' Pond," said Mrs Taylor. "People said it was haunted – haunted by the witches who drowned there. I never believed in all of that – I thought it was all nonsense – but I knew Vera did. I also knew that she hated to be made to look like she was scared of anything. She was the easiest person to set a dare for.

"So one day, I don't know why, but I dared her to swim in the Witches' Pond. All the village kids had been swimming in the river together. Vera ignored me, of course, but mostly it didn't matter because everyone was having such a great time.

"But on the way home, I bumped into her in the woods and she tried to ignore me again.

For some reason, I told her I was going to swim in the Witches' Pond. I don't know why I even thought of it. It just came into my head.

"She told me I wouldn't dare. I said I wasn't scared. It was her that was scared. It was her who wouldn't dare. I knew that would get her and it did. I don't know what it was about that day that made me go on at her. There was just something about how smug she looked – how much she seemed to enjoy ignoring me. Something just snapped inside me, I suppose."

"How do you mean?" said Rosie. "What snapped?"

Mrs Taylor pointed to her heart.

"In here," she said.

Then she pointed to her head.

"And in here."

Rosie frowned. She didn't understand.

"We still had our costumes on," continued Mrs Taylor. "It was such a lovely sunny day. I don't think Vera thought I'd do it, but I marched all the way to the Witches' Pond and jumped straight in. Vera had no choice other than to do the same or look a coward. So she did.

"As soon as she jumped in, I got out. The water wasn't just cold – I can't explain it. But it wasn't just that. I suddenly remembered all the stories about witches being drowned there. I could see it all so vividly in my head. I stood shivering on the bank, my heart racing.

"Vera looked back at me from the middle of the pond and laughed and called me a coward for getting out. The whole prank felt like it had gone wrong. To be honest, though, what Vera thought of me didn't matter any more.

"Vera took longer to realise how cold it was, but I saw her grin vanish as it took hold of her.

I could see the fear in her eyes too. She started to splash back to the bank, but she was slow and clumsy, and I saw her start to panic. She opened up her mouth to shout, but it filled with water and she started to choke. Her head went back as she tried to breathe ... Then she went under."

Rosie swallowed hard. Mrs Taylor's eyes were filled with tears.

"I could have jumped in to try and save her. But I couldn't. I just couldn't. Nothing would get me back in that water.

"I yelled, but it took ages for anyone to come," she went on. "Children first, but then they fetched the grown-ups. They found her body wrapped in weeds at the bottom ..."

Mrs Taylor shook her head. "Of course, I never told anyone what I'd done. I just said I'd seen her struggling and called for help. But Vera knew. Vera knows ..."

"What do you mean?" said Rosie.

"She's waiting for revenge," said Mrs Taylor.

"Revenge?" said Rosie. "What kind of revenge?"

"She's waiting for Mary," said Mrs Taylor. "That's why she wanted her to come to that pond. I think she's waiting for Mary so she can punish me by drowning her. Lord knows I deserve it!"

"Mary's at the mill pond!" said Rosie, jumping to her feet.

"What?" said Mrs Taylor. "But—"

"They've all gone. I promised you I wouldn't go and I promised them I wouldn't tell, but, oh, Mrs Taylor, I'm sorry."

But Mrs Taylor wasn't listening now. She was already in the hallway putting on her shoes.

Chapter 12

Vera

Mrs Taylor opened the door and ran off towards the Witches' Pond with Rosie not far behind, still trying to get one of her sandals on properly.

Rosie was quicker, though, and caught up with Mrs Taylor in the woods. They ran on together without saying a word until they came out of the trees and saw the Witches' Pond filled with laughing, splashing children. It was

so different to the still and silent place Rosie
had visited before.

Mrs Taylor paced the bank. She scanned
all the faces, frantically looking for Mary, and
as each child in turn saw her, they fell silent
apart from the odd one who shouted "Snitch!"
at Rosie, making her flinch.

Rosie and Mrs Taylor both saw Mary at
the same time. She was fine and looked both
alarmed and annoyed to have been caught.
Mrs Taylor shrieked wildly and beckoned for
her to come to the bank – to come out of the
water.

Mary was clearly embarrassed by her
mother shouting at her, but she and all the
children there began to get frightened too,
and Mary – and the others – started to move
towards her mother. It was then that Rosie saw
the girl behind Mary. It was the girl she'd seen
before – the ghost girl. It was Vera.

Mrs Taylor saw her too.

"Vera!" she yelled. "Vera, no!"

Mary turned to see who her mother was looking at but could clearly see no one at all. *Maybe Vera can decide who sees her and who can't*, thought Rosie. *Maybe all ghosts can.*

"Vera!" shouted Mrs Taylor. "I'm sorry. I'm sorry. Please! Please don't hurt her. It's not her fault."

Vera just smiled, her eyes shining, and began to move slowly and silently, like an otter, towards Mary, who was never going to reach the bank before Vera caught up with her.

Mrs Taylor threw herself into the water and thrashed noisily towards her daughter.

"Get out!" she screamed at Mary. "Get out!"

Mary swam towards the bank, as did all the other children. They scrambled out of the water as though it was suddenly boiling hot and threw themselves onto the grass, gasping and shouting. Soon there was just Mrs Taylor alone in the centre of the pond. The air became still.

"Vera!" Mrs Taylor yelled, slapping the water. "I'm sorry! I'm sorry!"

She put her hands to her face and sobbed. The children stared on in silence. There was total confusion. Mary started crying. Rosie became aware that everything was going dark again, as if a shadow was passing across the pond, even though there was not one single cloud in the sky.

Then, with horrifying suddenness, Mrs Taylor was pulled under.

The violence of it was shocking. She just vanished. A whirlpool was the only evidence that she had even been there, and that closed up quickly.

Then she thrust an arm up through the surface, the hand grasping at the air. The children gasped as she was pulled under for a second, final time.

All was still again. It seemed an age before Mary screamed.

Chapter 13

Back to London

Rosie stared out of the window of the vicar's house. There was a breeze moving through the treetops. Rosie imagined it rippling the surface of the Witches' Pond.

She closed her eyes and remembered standing staring while help arrived, two men jumping in the water to search for Mrs Taylor, pulling her lifeless body towards the bank and hauling it out, Mary screaming and screaming.

The children all around were crying, but Rosie just stood and stared at the water that now grew calm again, like a wound healing over. She had to be pulled away by Miss Baxter and felt like she was sleepwalking. Nothing seemed quite real.

It took hours for the shock of it all to sink in, and then Rosie kept having flashbacks of Mrs Taylor's face just as she was dragged under. Rosie knew she would never forget how she had looked – her eyes wide, her mouth open in a scream she would not have the time to make.

Rosie hoped Mrs Taylor was at least free now. She would not feel guilty every day. Maybe she was finally at peace. Not that this thought helped Mary, who blamed Rosie for bringing her mother to the pond. Nothing could comfort her. Rosie would never forget the look on Mary's face either as Miss Baxter had led Rosie away. It was a look of absolute hatred.

Rosie could not stay there. Everyone was being very nice, but they all understood that. Rosie heard them whispering and planning, and wondered where she would go next. After two days at the vicarage, they told Rosie that they had contacted her mother and that she had caught the next train.

Rosie wanted to see her mother so much. She sat watching the hands of the clock on the shelf, willing them to turn faster, while Miss Baxter stood fidgeting by the bookcase. Finally, Rosie heard a knock at the door.

"Mum!" shouted Rosie, pushing past the vicar and Miss Baxter to hug her.

"Careful!" said her mother. "You almost knocked me over!"

But then they just hugged and hugged and hugged, and Rosie closed her eyes and imagined they were in London.

"Shall we go home?" said Rosie's mother, as if she could read her mind.

"What, London?" said Rosie.

"Well, I don't know how many homes you've got. Of course London."

"Yes!" said Rosie. "Yes, please."

"We'll take our chances together, eh?" said Rosie's mother.

Rosie smiled.

"We will," she said.

The vicar did not seem to approve of Rosie's mother taking her back to London. But then he probably didn't approve of London either, and that was just fine with Rosie.

After tea and sandwiches, Rosie packed her case and thanked the vicar and the vicar's wife for looking after her. Miss Baxter came out onto the doorstep to wish them well and tell Rosie's mother – between coughs – what a lovely girl Rosie was. They wished her luck and waved goodbye, and Rosie and her mother set off for the station.

Rosie wanted to tell her mother about Mrs Taylor and Vera, but she did not know how to start. Maybe she would tell her one day. When the war was over, maybe.

"I mean, don't get me wrong," said Rosie's mother, looking around as they walked. "It's lovely and all that. Pretty and everything. But I couldn't live here. Not for all the tea in China. Something about it gives me the creeps. I know I sound daft."

"No, Mum," said Rosie. "Not daft at all."

It felt like a very long time since Rosie had arrived with the other evacuees and lined up on the station platform, but it was only a few days. She never thought she would ever have longed so much for London, but she wanted more than anything to be back in her own bed.

"Old Mr Garside down the road says it's all a load of nonsense," said Rosie's mother as they stood on the platform. "He reckons there never will be any bombs. He says they'd be crazy to bomb us, because we'd only go and bomb them back."

Rosie smiled. She wanted to believe that, but Mr Garside was a grumpy old man who always wanted to seem like he knew more than anyone else about everything. *Still*, she thought. *Maybe this time he is right.*

They heard the train before they saw it. They heard the whistle and then saw the plume of steam over some trees.

"Here we are," said Rosie's mother. "We'll be home before you know it."

The train huffed and puffed as it wheezed out of the station, and Rosie's mother put her arm around her and pulled her close. The train slowly passed by the outskirts of the village. Soon the whole place and everything that happened there would be like a dream.

"Looks awful quiet, don't it?" said Rosie's mother.

Rosie smiled.

"Yes," said Rosie. "Awful quiet."

"You taking the mickey out me, girl?" said her mother.

She snuggled into her mother.

"As if I would," said Rosie.

Rosie looked out of the window and sat up as she realised that they were going to go past the mill pond. A cloud of steam hid the view for a moment and when it cleared, Rosie gasped.

"What is it, Rosie?" said her mother. "Is that the pond where ...? Oh, Rosie, it's all right."

Rosie's mother hugged her tightly, and Rosie peeked out towards the window as the last of the village buildings gave way to open fields.

But it had not been the sight of the Witches' Pond that had given Rosie a fright. It was seeing, standing at the top of the bank leading to the pond, two girls looking out at the passing train, looking straight at Rosie.

One of the girls was Vera. It took Rosie a little longer to work out who the other one was. Then she saw it was Mrs Taylor – or Mrs Taylor when she was a girl.

Vera had not been waiting for Mary at all, thought Rosie. *She had been waiting for Mrs Taylor. Every lonely day for all those years.*

Maybe she had been waiting for Rosie too. Waiting for Rosie to bring Mrs Taylor to the pond – waiting for all the moments that had just passed to line up, just so. It was just like Mrs Taylor had said. Now she and Vera were friends again.

Friends for ever.

Our books are tested
for children and young people by
children and young people.

Thanks to everyone who consulted on
a manuscript for their time and effort in
helping us to make our books better
for our readers.